Introduction

Although clinical depression is often thought of as an adult disease, it can affect children as well. Unfortunately, children may not have the maturity to understand what is happening to them, or they may feel powerless to change their situation, so they don't speak up about what they are going through. It is up to adults to be on the lookout for signs of trouble and to recognize when a child needs help.

What to Watch For – Potential Warning Signs of Depression in Children:

Sadness, hopelessness, loss of pleasure or interest, anxiety, turmoil (anger outbursts)

Difficulty organizing thoughts (concentrating), extreme negativity, worthlessness and guilt, helplessness, feelings of isolation, thoughts of suicide

Changes in appetite or weight, sleep disturbances, sluggishness, agitation

Avoidance and withdrawal, clingy and demanding behavior, excessive activity, restlessness, self-harm

What to do:

- Don't minimize your child's feelings. Reassure your child that depression is not something to be ashamed about – Some people have a hard time recovering from being sad.
- Work hard to cultivate trust and communication with your child and be aware of the impact your own responses in life are having on your child. You are your child's coping instructor.
- Allow your child the right to feel depressed and teach him/her that asking for help is ok – If he/she thinks depression is bad or not ok, he/she may try to hide his/her feelings from you.
- Tell your child the truth and give him/her time to grieve. By being honest, you are allowing your child to work through the pain.
- Pay attention to the length of your child's symptoms. If the symptoms linger for an extended period of time, or if you see severe changes in your child's personality, seek professional help.
- Although suicide in children is rare, it does happen. Take it very seriously if your child says or acts like he wants to die.

If your child is experiencing frequent signs of depression that last for extended periods of time, it is crucial that you seek professional help. Children who are experiencing signs of depression do not automatically need medication. Many children will respond to therapy alone. If you are uncertain where to seek help, contact your child's school counselor or your family physician for a referral.

National Center for Youth Issues
Practical Guidance Resources Educators Can Trust
ncyi.org

P.O. Box 22185 • Chattanooga, TN 37422-2185 • 423.899.5714 • 800.477.8277 • fax: 423.899.4547 • www.ncyi.org
ISBN: 978-1-937870-05-8 • © 2012 National Center for Youth Issues, Chattanooga, TN • All rights reserved.

Summary: A supplementary teacher's guide for *Blueloon.*
Full of discussion questions and exercises to share with students.

Written by: Julia Cook • Contributing Editor: Sarah I. Springer • Illustrations by: Anita DuFalla
Published by National Center for Youth Issues

Printed at Starkey Printing • Chattanooga, TN, USA • April 2013

Stress Charades

Objectives

• Identify things that make you feel stressed out.
• Visualize stressors by acting them out.
• Recognize that others experience stress.
• Learn alternative coping strategies for handling stress.

Materials

• Paper
• Paper Strips (5 per Student)
• Large container

Directions

1. Make a list of all of the things that stress you out on a sheet of paper.

2. Select your top five stressors from the list and circle them.

3. Copy each of your five stressors onto strips of paper and fold them up.

4. Place your folded strips into a jar or container along with everyone else's and mix up.

Divide your group into two teams. Have the first member of Team One draw a strip from the jar and act out that stressor for his/her team. If a teammate guesses the stressor, then Team One gets the point. If after 90 seconds, Team One has not guessed correctly, Team Two can gather together, discuss an answer and make one guess. If they get it correct, then Team Two gets a point. Write the stressor that was drawn on the board for all to see. Next have Team Two draw a strip and repeat the process. The first team to five points wins.

Once a winner is determined, review all of the stressors that were used in the game.

As a group, discuss effective ways to counteract them.

3

My Own

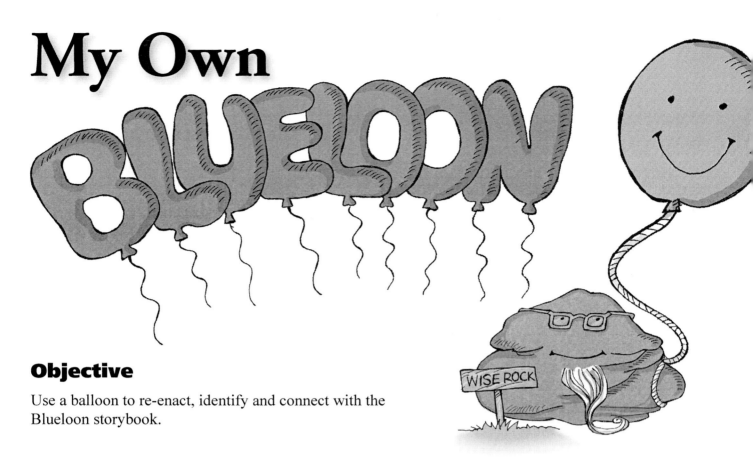

Objective

Use a balloon to re-enact, identify and connect with the Blueloon storybook.

Directions

1. Blow up balloons and close them with a twisty tie. (This will make it possible to let air out and blow more air in.)

2. Tie a string to each balloon.

3. Divide the balloon into thirds as shown (Fig. 1). Draw 3 faces on each balloon (sad face, happy face, and neutral face.)

4. Play with the balloon as you act out and discuss the Blueloon storybook.

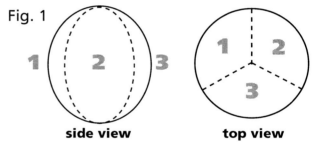

Fig. 1

side view   top view

Materials

- One round balloon for each person
- One wire baggie tie for each balloon
- One piece of string for each balloon
- Black Magic Marker

The Goal Chain

Objective

Develop a realization that setting small, related, attainable goals is significant when trying to reach bigger goals. When reaching the bigger goal seems overwhelming, break it up into smaller parts.

Materials

- (2) 5"x 8" index cards per person
- Sheet of paper
- Pencils or markers
- Multi-colored paper strips 3/4" wide and 6 inches long.
- Scissors or an Exacto knife
- Stapler or glue

Directions

1. Make a 1" x 1/8" slit in the middle of the right edge of one of the 5"x 8" cards as shown (A).
2. Repeat with the other 5"x 8" card in the middle of the left side.
3. On the 5"x 8" card with the slit on the right, draw a picture of where you are in life now.
4. On the 5"x 8" card with the slit on the left, draw a picture of where you would like to be.
5. On the sheet of paper, make a list of all of the things you need to do/accomplish that will help you get where you want to be.
6. Write down each thing on a different colored strip of paper.
7. Connect the first strip to the 5"x 8" card (through the slit) and glue or staple the ends together (B).
8. Attach the other strips to the first strip, attaching the final strip to the 5"x 8" card with the slit on the left (C).
9. You now have a visual for what it takes to get from where you are to where you want to be!
10. Discuss how each link in the chain is important and necessary.

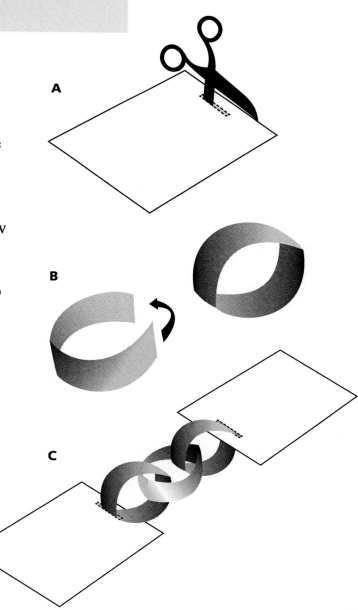

A

B

C

Goal Pizza Pie

Materials
• Pencil
• Markers
• Scissors
• White Paper

Objective

Help people avoid the "whole pie" syndrome.
Identify small steps for success.

Directions

1. Draw three circles using a seperate sheet of paper for each. The first circle will be whole (A), the second divided in thirds (B) and the third circle divided by sixths (C). Cut out the whole circle and the parts to each of the other two circles. Set aside.

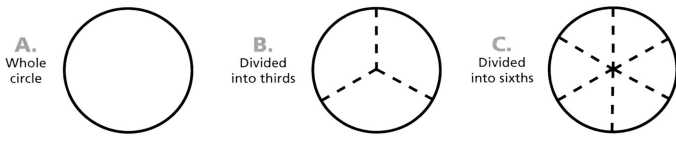

A. Whole circle

B. Divided into thirds

C. Divided into sixths

2. Write down an achievable ultimate goal that you would like to achieve in the top box of the flow chart below (A).

3. Write down three medium-sized goals that will help you accomplish your ultimate achievable goal in the next three boxes (B).

4. Write down two small goals that will help you accomplish each of your three medium-sized goals in the boxes (C).

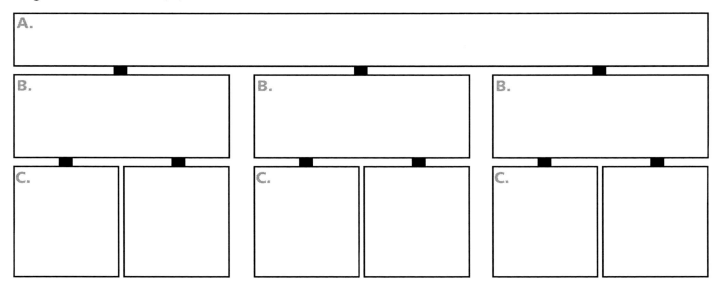

5. Draw a picture of your ultimate achievable goal and label it on the whole circle paper.

6. Draw pictures of each of the 3 medium-sized goals and label them on the 1/3 circle pieces.

7. Draw pictures of each of the small goals and label them on the 1/6 circle pieces.

Use this pizza model to visualize that your big goals are easiest to achieve and accomplish if you can break them down into smaller goals. Just like pizza…it's hard to eat the whole thing in one sitting. Eating one small piece at a time makes it much easier!

Healthy Habits

Objective
Recognize the value of healthy habits. Identify ten healthy habits that are important to you.

Materials
- Interview sheet
- Pencil or pen
- Person figure pattern
- Scissors
- Markers, pens and pencils

Directions

1. Interview five people and ask them to list ten healthy habits that are important in life (use form on next page).

2. Take your list of 50 healthy habits and condense it into one master list (length will vary.)

3. Select ten healthy habits from your condensed list that are most important to you, and write them with a marker on the person figure on right. This represents your top ten written on YOU!

4. Select your favorite healthy habit from your list and answer the following questions on a piece of paper:
   a. What is your healthy habit?
   b. Why is it important?
   c. What can happen if you do not practice this healthy habit?
   d. What are you going to do to make sure that you do practice this healthy habit?

5. Present your person figure to the rest of the group.

6. Display for all to see.

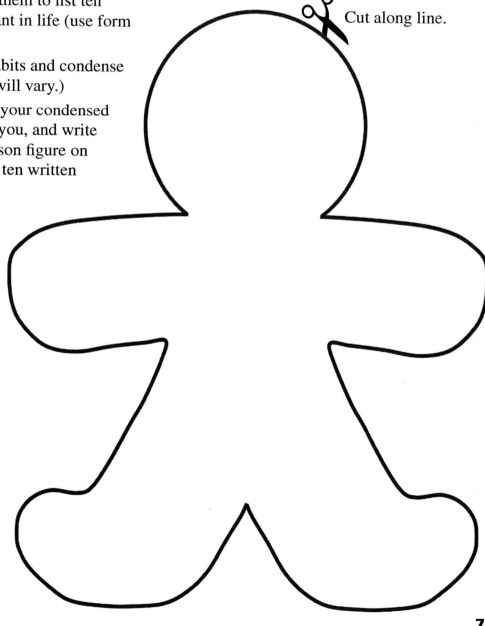

Cut along line.

PERSON ONE

Habit 1: _____
Habit 2: _____
Habit 3: _____
Habit 4: _____
Habit 5: _____
Habit 6: _____
Habit 7: _____
Habit 8: _____
Habit 9: _____
Habit 10: _____

PERSON TWO

Habit 1: _____
Habit 2: _____
Habit 3: _____
Habit 4: _____
Habit 5: _____
Habit 6: _____
Habit 7: _____
Habit 8: _____
Habit 9: _____
Habit 10: _____

PERSON THREE

Habit 1: _____
Habit 2: _____
Habit 3: _____
Habit 4: _____
Habit 5: _____
Habit 6: _____
Habit 7: _____
Habit 8: _____
Habit 9: _____
Habit 10: _____

PERSON FOUR

Habit 1: _____
Habit 2: _____
Habit 3: _____
Habit 4: _____
Habit 5: _____
Habit 6: _____
Habit 7: _____
Habit 8: _____
Habit 9: _____
Habit 10: _____

PERSON FIVE

Habit 1: _____
Habit 2: _____
Habit 3: _____
Habit 4: _____
Habit 5: _____
Habit 6: _____
Habit 7: _____
Habit 8: _____
Habit 9: _____
Habit 10: _____

The "I" CAN

Objective

When you can recognize what your **"I can's"** are, your **"I can'ts"** don't seem quite as overwhelming!

Materials
- One clean empty soup can
- Construction paper
- Markers and/or colored pencils
- 4-5 small items that can fit inside your can.

Directions

1. Cover cans with construction paper.
2. Write the words "I CAN!" on the side of the can and decorate any way you want.
3. Fill your can with five items that represent things that you "CAN" do (items that can represent your talents and/or abilities.)
4. Take turns with other group members sharing the items in the can. Start each explanation with "I can ….."
5. After everyone has shared, have each person in the group comment on at least one "I CAN" from other members in the group.

NOTE: This activity can also help people develop greater respect for one another, good listening skills, and self-control.

Mirror, Mirror

Objective
We need to be our own best friend and not so hard on ourselves.

Materials
- Small mirror
- Paper
- Pencil

Directions

1. Take out a piece of paper.
2. Divide your paper in half lengthwise and write positive (+) at the top of one side and negative (-) at the top of the other side.
3. Think about all of the things (both positive and negative) that you can say about yourself, and write them down on the sheet.
4. Look at your (-) list and ask yourself if you would feel comfortable saying these same things out loud to someone else. If you wouldn't, you need to stop being so hard on yourself.
5. Look in the mirror and practice saying all of your positives to yourself! Remember…you can't expect other people to like you if you don't like yourself! Positive Self-Talk ROCKS!!!

Sense of Balance

Materials
- 10 identical sized tissue boxes
- (2) oversized plain T-shirts
- Fabric Paint or Permanent Marker

Objective
You can't be everything to everyone all the time; you need a healthy sense of balance in life and in all that you do.

Directions
- Write the words "Just Getting By" on one of the T-shirts and "My Personal Best" on the other.
- Have two people put on the shirts and stand side by side.
- Give each person 5 tissue boxes to hold.
- Explain that each tissue box represents 10% of your day.
- Explain that if 50% of the time you are "Just Getting By" and 50% of the time you are doing your "Personal Best," you are officially coasting through life.
- Take one tissue box from the "Just Getting By" person and hand it to the "My Personal Best" person.
- Explain that if more often you are doing your personal best than just getting by, you are being a **producer**.
- Take two tissue boxes away from the "My Personal Best" person and hand them to the "Just Getting By" person.
- Explain that if more often you are just getting by in life, rather than doing your personal best, you are being a **consumer**.
- Place all 10 tissue boxes in the hands of the "My Personal Best" person and explain that trying to be all things to all people all of the time can be unhealthy.
- Place all 10 tissue boxes in the hands of the "Just Getting By" person and explain that doing nothing and having everyone do everything for you can also be unhealthy.
- Move the tissue boxes back and forth, and explain that being a 60/40, 70/30, or 80/20 producer is great, but encourage people to stay away from 90/10 or 100/0.
- Explain the detriments that go along with being a 20/80, 30/70, or 40/60 consumer.
- Everyone will have days (or times) when he/she will act like a **consumer** and a **coaster**, but if you try to be a producer more of the time, you will "WIN" at life.

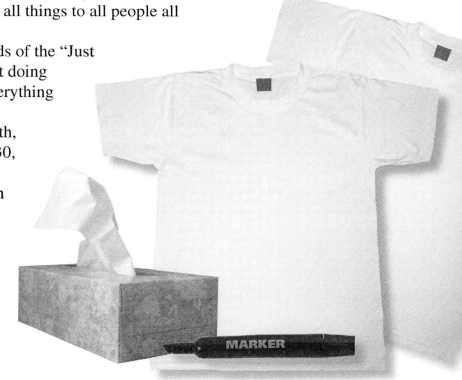

10

The Negative Thought Log

Objective

Counteract negative thinking and recognize that our moods affect the way we view the world. It may not be as bad as it seems at the time.

Directions

1. Whenever you have a negative (-) thought, write it down on the left side of the chart.
2. Write down what you feel is causing this negative (-) thinking on the right side of the chart.
3. The next time you are in a positive mood (+), look at the chart and see if your negative thought was truly warranted.

Negative Thoughts	What is Causing Me to Think this Way?

Weathering Your Thoughts

Materials
- Different pictures of different types of weather (Sunny, Rainy, Windy, Stormy, Rainbow, etc.)
- Worksheet below
- Pencils
- Markers or crayons
- Construction paper

Objective

Associate different feelings and thoughts with different kinds of weather. Although you can't control the weather, you can control the "weather" that's in your mind.

Directions:

1. Using the chart below, write down 3-4 feelings that you would associate with each weather pattern (i.e. sunny = happy, rainy = sad, thunder and lightning= scared, etc.)

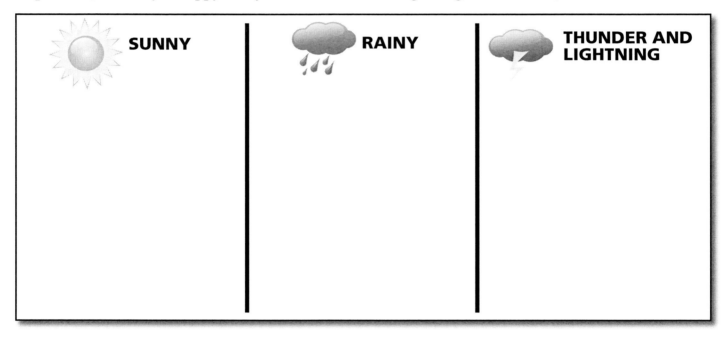

SUNNY	RAINY	THUNDER AND LIGHTNING

2. Think about your day and answer the following questions:

    a. What was the best thing that happened to you today?

        i. What type of weather best describes how you felt during this time?

        ii. Draw a picture of this type of weather.

    b. What was the worst thing that happened to you today?

        i. What type of weather best describes how you felt during this time?

        ii. Draw a picture of this type of weather.

    c. Did you have any challenging moments today?

        i. If so, make a list below.

1. What type of weather best describes how you felt during each challenging situation?

2. Draw a picture of the weather during each of today's challenging moments.

3. What can you do to help change the "weather" inside your head during a challenging situation? (What can you do to make a rainy day sunny?)

How Full is Your Water Bottle?

Objective

Recognize your own level of self-worth.

Materials

- Empty 20 ounce water bottle
- Water colored with red food coloring
- Measuring cup or cup with pour spout
- Paper and pencil
- Sharpie Marker

Directions

1. Draw ten equally spaced lines on the widest part of the water bottle.

2. Fill the measuring cup with water and add food coloring.

3. Write down ten things about yourself on paper, starting with at least two positive things.

4. For every positive thing on your list, fill the water bottle up one line.

5. For every negative thing on your list, pour out one line of water.

6. Do this every day for five days and compare your levels.

7. What are some things that you can do to get your water bottle more full?

"Masking" the Whole Truth

Objective

We all have feelings that we are willing and able to express to others and those that we keep inside of ourselves. This activity will help us to identify our inside feelings and express our emotions in productive ways.

Directions

1. Decorate your first mask with all of the feelings that you allow others to see on a daily basis.
2. Decorate the second mask with your "inside" feelings that others do not usually see.
3. Talk about each mask and the challenges associated with expressing your inside feelings to others.
4. Discuss what it was like to share your inside feelings with someone else.

Materials
- Two plastic or cardboard masks (per person)
- Markers

Cheers for Peers

Objective

People often find it easier to help others, rather than talking about their own needs. This activity gives people an opportunity to identify and suggest strategies that others can use to help them feel happier.

Directions

1. Brainstorm positive things that you might suggest to a friend who is feeling sad, mad, angry, hurt, etc…
2. Select your top ten suggestions and the reasons why you have chosen them.
3. Write these top choices on the ten strips of paper, and place them in the shoe box.
4. Decorate the "Cheers for Peers" helping box, and select an area of the room to keep it for the next person who may need some cheers.

Materials
- Shoebox
- Strips of blank paper about two inches wide (ten per person)
- Pencil

"Where in the World are..."

Objective

Identify people in our lives who provide us with support.

Materials

- Large map of the world
- Copies of seven (or more) cutout people

Directions

People in various parts of our inner world provide us with different levels of support.

1. Brainstorm at least seven people in your life that you can go to for support.

2. Decorate the cutout images in a way that reflects each person's personality and physical characteristics.

3. Place a cutout image in each of the seven continents based on how much you rely on each person. The farther the person is placed in distance, the less likely you are to rely on them daily.

4. Discuss why people were placed in different areas on the map.

5. Write down ways that each person contributes to your life in positive ways.

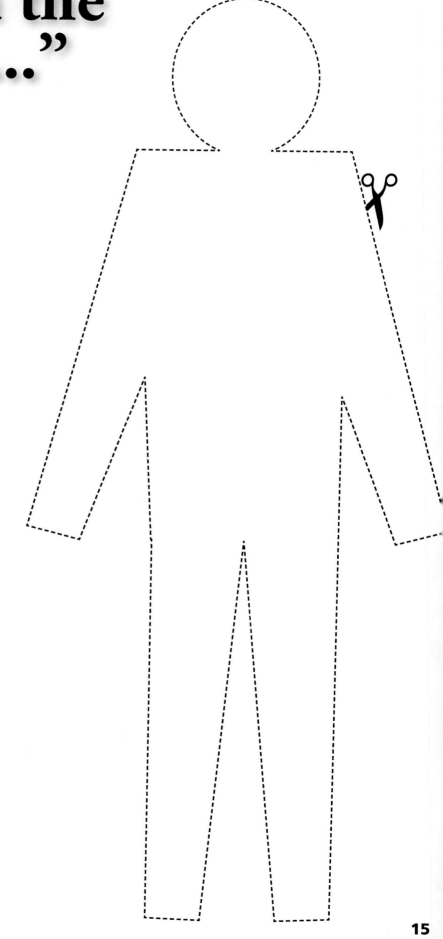

"Organizing" My Achievements

Objective

People who are experiencing feelings of depression often have difficulty focusing and staying organized. This activity will provide an opportunity to create a collage of positive achievements and interests that can be utilized as both a helpful organizational tool and reminder of positive self-talk.

Materials

- Magazines
- Scissors
- Scotch tape
- One organizational tool for each person (e.g. pencil box/ folder/binder, etc.)

Directions

1. Search through magazines and images that remind you of something positive in your life. This may be an achievement (someone swimming a race), a place that makes you feel happy (the beach), or something of interest (movie stars or a cake to represent baking, etc.).

2. Once these images are cut out, discuss which organizational tool you want to design as a reminder of these positive images. (If a person is struggling to write down homework, you might consider decorating a planner or folder. If a person is not struggling with organization, you might choose an organizational tool that is most visible to you during the day, so that you are regularly reminded of these pictures).

3. Decorate the organizational tools and discuss how each picture contributes to one positive aspect of your life.

"Reframing" Your Blue Shades

Objective

Reframing negative thoughts

Materials
- Two cut-out pairs of paper eye glasses
- Blue cellophane
- Tape
- Scissors

Directions

1. Cut out two pairs of paper eye glasses.

2. Tape blue cellophane over both lenses of one pair of glasses.

3. Indicate that when you look through the pair with blue lenses, you are thinking negatively. Give an example of negative thoughts that have been shared with you (e.g. I will never understand math, etc.).

4. Ask students to then put on the frames with the clear lenses and "reframe" that thought into something positive (e.g. When I have trouble with math, I know that I can ask Mr. _____ for help).

5. Repeat this activity using personal examples of negativity to help encourage the practice of reframing negative self-talk.

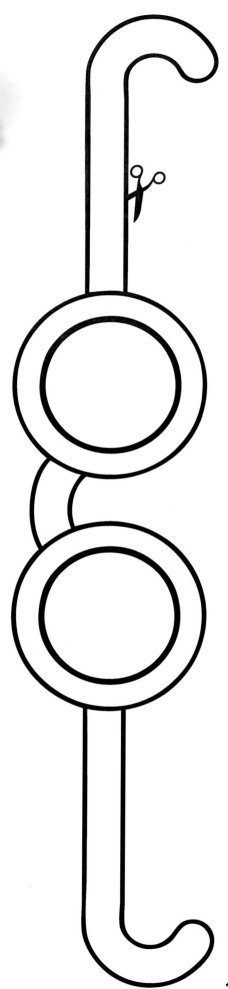

Wall of Heroes

Objective

People we choose to surround ourselves with can help us to stand tall and overcome challenges. This activity will help us to identify specific individuals in our lives who help and encourage us to be our best.

Directions

1. Brainstorm individuals who have had a positive influence on your life.

2. Choose one individual in your life for each prompt below, and complete the sentence.

3. Draw a picture of yourself standing tall and confident in the middle circle. If possible, laminate the picture and hang it on your wall to help remind you of your "wall of heroes."

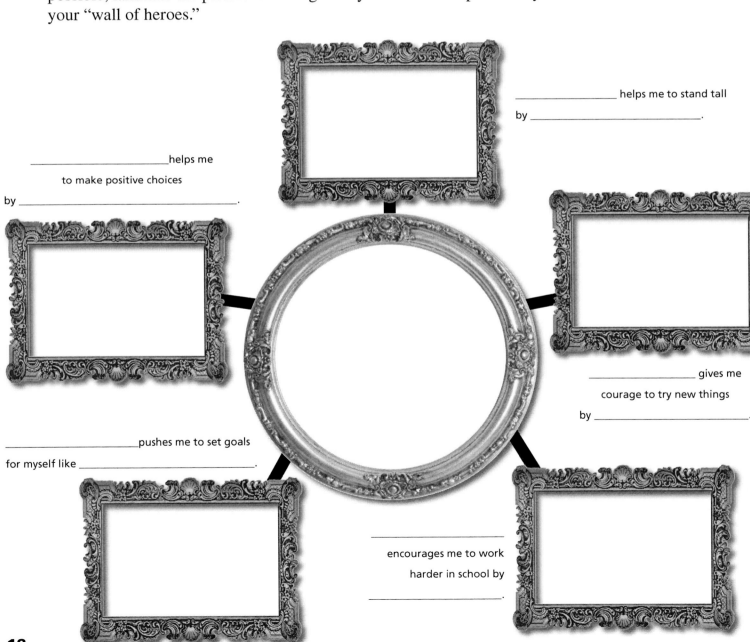

_____ helps me to stand tall by _____.

_____ helps me to make positive choices by _____.

_____ gives me courage to try new things by _____.

_____ pushes me to set goals for myself like _____.

_____ encourages me to work harder in school by _____.

Living in the Moment

Objective

Identify current personal attributes and discuss goals for the future.

Directions

1. "You can't change the past, but you can ruin the present by worrying about the future." – Isak Dinesen

    a. Write down what this quote means to you.

_____

_____

2. What are you doing today to be: A better friend than last year?

_____

_____

3. What are you doing today to be: A stronger student/professional than last year?

_____

_____

4. What are you doing today to be: A more helpful son/daughter than last year?

_____

_____

5. What can I start doing tomorrow to become an even better friend?

_____

_____

6. What can I start doing tomorrow to become an even stronger student/professional?

_____

_____

7. What can I start doing tomorrow to become an even more helpful son/daughter?

_____

_____

8. Circle one of these goals to specifically work on in the next month.

    a. Here are the steps I am going to take to reach this goal:

        i. _____

        ii. _____

        iii. _____

    b. I'll know I've reached my goal when:

_____

_____

The Power of Three Contract

Objective

Identify healthy eating, sleeping, and exercise patterns that can increase positive feelings.

Directions

Food for "Thought"

It is important to choose healthy foods that will give me brain power to focus and do my best.

Here are some healthy foods that I enjoy:

_____

_____

Here is a healthy food I am willing to try _____ .

Sleep to "Leap"

Getting the right amount of sleep (8-10 hrs per night) is important in helping me to be healthy and feel better. Too little or too much sleep will not allow me to be at my best.

I usually get _____ (amount) of hours of sleep per night. If it is not between 8 and 10 hours in the next week, I will make a plan with my family to work on achieving this goal.

Dive to "Thrive"

Exercise helps my body to function better and increases my chances of having a positive attitude at the same time.

Here are the things I am currently doing to get exercise:

_____

_____

Here is another form of exercise I am willing to try:

_____

_____

_____

SIGNATURE OF STUDENT

_____

SIGNATURE OF PARENT

_____

SIGNATURE OF COUNSELOR

Raining Feelings

Objective

When we feel deflated, we often find ourselves expressing anger. Anger is an "umbrella" feeling that usually has many other feelings underneath it. This activity will help us to work on developing emotional expression skills by recognizing that our current behavior may be an expression of many different feelings that can be addressed independently.

Directions

Fill in and discuss the following prompts:

1. When I get angry, I express it by _____

   _____.

2. When I feel deflated, my umbrella leaks: (Circle all of the emotions under the umbrella that I experience when I feel deflated).

3. When I feel _____(write in circled feeling), here is something I can do to help myself feel better _____.

4. When I feel _____ (write in a second circled feeling), here is something else I can do to help me feel better _____

   _____.

5. Repeat as needed for each circled emotion.

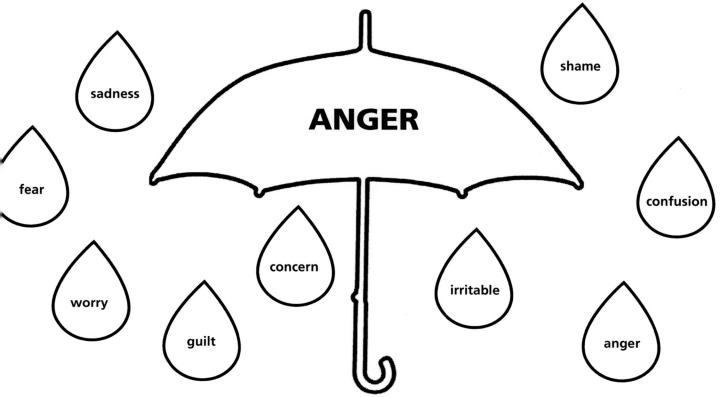

What's Your Take?

Objective
Identify multiple perspectives on a given situation.

Directions

1. What do you see when you look at a glass that has water filled up to the halfway point?

2. Discuss the difference between a half-full glass verses a half-empty glass perspective.
   a. When we think negatively, we often can't see alternative perspectives.

3. Look at the pictures (below) and try to identify or distinguish between both images.
   a. Remember that there is not a "right or wrong" way of looking at something – it's just different!

Illusion 1
Old or Young?

1959, W.E. Hill

Illusion 2
Face or Vase?

Illusion 3
Which Black Dot is Larger?

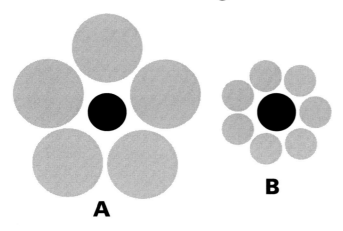

A   B

Illusion 4
Which is Larger?

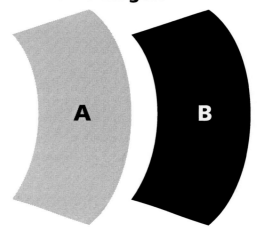

A   B

Circling Compliments

Objective

We are not often taught the language and/or encouraged to verbally provide positive feedback to our peers. In turn, we struggle to receive positive feedback. This activity provides some prompts that can be utilized in a group setting to encourage positive feedback exchanges.

Directions

This activity may be especially effective when used at the end of any kind of group meeting as a way to wrap up the session.

1. People will begin sitting in a circle and are introduced to several prompts (below) that they can use to support their peers. A brainstorming session may be utilized to identify additional prompts that represent times where one might catch others making good choices.

2. People will then be encouraged to go around the circle individually and share a compliment for someone in the group. The compliments need to be specific and if possible, unique to each person.

    a. All people must give and receive a compliment. The person giving the compliment must look at the person he/she is talking to and speak loudly enough for everyone to hear the compliment.

If this activity is repeated after each meeting, students are likely to spend more time observing positive character traits throughout the day, contributing to a more positive group culture.

Variation of this activity: (Might be used during a final group meeting)

People are asked to write down a compliment for each person on individual index cards. They are then instructed to give each person in the group a compliment card. When each person has received a compliment from everyone in the group, they can then use the note cards to create a wall of compliments to be laminated and posted in a special place.

Prompts:

I am proud of _____ because during _____,
              name of person   name of activity

I noticed _____.
                                     observation

_____ showed respect for his peers by:_____.
        name of person

_____ helped a classmate by: _____.
        name of person

My Invisible Suitcase

Directions

Everyone has an invisible suitcase.

1. If you go on a trip, think of other words that someone might use to describe a suitcase. (You might suggest the place you pick up your suitcase in an airport – the "baggage" claim) Another word for suitcase is, "baggage." Each person's suitcase (or baggage) influences how he/she thinks, feels and acts in a given situation.

2. Think about a time that something great happened to you, like scoring a goal in soccer. Describe or draw how you felt after this positive experience.

3. Now, think of a time that something not so great happened, like you had an argument with someone before coming to school or work. Describe or draw how you felt and acted after that experience.

4. Because each person's suitcase is invisible, we don't know what experiences, thoughts and feelings people bring with them each day. Often times, we take things out on others when we are upset about something else. Perhaps you have yelled at someone after you received a bad grade on a test. Draw or write about a time when something like this happened to you.

My Invisible Suitcase
(continued)

5. Draw a picture of something currently in your invisible suitcase that is weighing you down.

6. Describe how your invisible suitcase is affecting your relationships with others (parents, friends, teachers/colleagues, etc.) by following the prompts below.

    a. When I have _____ in my invisible suitcase, my friends/parents feel….

    b. When I have _____ in my invisible suitcase, my teachers/colleagues don't….

7. On tough days when you have a lot of stress, if you could lock your suitcase up and store it away, where would you keep it? Draw a picture of where this place would be.

8. Vacation time! When you are ready to unpack your invisible suitcase, where would you go in your life that might help fill your suitcase with positive feelings and memories? Draw a picture of a place that makes you feel comfortable, safe and happy (e.g. grandparents' house, bedroom, soccer field, beach, etc). Make sure to add pictures of the people that might help you to "unpack."

The Brain Bubble

Objective

Everyone has a brain bubble that starts talking the moment we notice or encounter something. The thoughts in our brain bubble can affect how we think and in addition, how we behave. If we can change our thoughts, we can have more control over the way we feel and ultimately act.

Directions:

"Hallway Merge"

You are walking down the hall and someone bumps into you...

1. Complete the worksheet below discussing each answer with the facilitator.

    a. If you think it is an accident, how do you think you would feel? Write it here. _____
_____

    b. If you think it is an accident, and you feel this way, how do you think you will act towards that person? Write it here. _____
_____

    c. Let's say you think it has been done on purpose. How do you think you would feel? Write it here. _____
_____

    d. If you think it has been done on purpose and you feel this way, how do you think you might act towards that person? Explain here. _____
_____

    e. Let's say a friend comes down the hall and says, "What's up?" with a smile on his face and playfully bumps you to say hello. How do you think you would feel? Write it here. _____
_____

    f. If you think that it has been done playfully, how do you think you will act towards that person? Write it here._____
_____

2. Compare your answers above and discuss the following: The same event happened each time with someone bumping into you, but the way your brain bubble thought about it determined how you felt and how you acted.

3. In the next portion of the activity, independently write down two ways of thinking about each situation and how it would change how the person might feel and act. Try looking at something with a half-empty glass and then a half-full glass to consider different perspectives.

"The T-shirt"

Someone likes your shirt and then wears the same outfit as you the following week.

• Here is an example of a "half–empty thought" _____
_____

The Brain Bubble (continued)

• How would you feel if you thought that way? _____

_____

• How might you act if you felt that way? _____

_____

• Here is an example of a "half–full thought" _____

• How would you feel if you thought that way? _____

• How would you act if you felt that way? _____

_____

"The Kickball Game"

You ask to play kickball at recess, and your peer walks away.

• Here is an example of a "half empty thought" _____

_____

• How would you feel if you thought that way? _____

_____

• How might you act if you felt that way? _____

_____

• Here is an example of a "half–full thought" _____

_____

• How would you feel if you thought that way? _____

_____

• How would you act if you felt that way? _____

_____

"The Slumber Party"

You invite friends to a sleepover, and five of the six friends have to leave by 10:00 pm.

• Here is an example of a "half empty thought" _____

_____

• How would you feel if you thought that way? _____

_____

• How might you act if you felt that way? _____

_____

• Here is an example of a "half–full thought" _____

_____

• How would you feel if you thought that way? _____

_____

• How would you act if you felt that way? _____

Bridging the Gap

Objective

There are many different life roles that make up our identities. This activity gives us an opportunity to identify any discrepancies between our current and "ideal" self.

Directions

We all have many life jobs like being a student/professional, son/daughter, trombone player, lacrosse player, etc.

1. Brainstorm your life jobs here. ▶

2. Circle three of these life jobs and begin by drawing a picture of what they currently look like.

3. In the blanks under each picture, label how you feel (physically and/or mentally).

4. Here is what I wish to look like:

Draw your **current** self here.

Draw your **ideal** self here.

5. Discuss the differences between both pictures.

6. Under the bridge, identify three small goals that you can set to bridge the gap between your current self and your ideal self.